IN LIEU OF A MEMOIR

A novelette

TADHG MULLER

First Published in 2019
by Open Pen, 25 Crescent Road, London, E13 0LU
openpen.co.uk
9781916413658
OPNOV005

OPEN PEN NOVELETTES #4
"In Lieu of a Memoir"
First Edition
© Tadhg Muller
Cover illustration by Pierre Buttin - pierrebuttin.com
© Pierre Buttin

Printed by Clays.

Introduction from the Editor

The notes that permeate the short stories within this novelette relate to the author accredited to this book, Tadhg Muller. Muller is a writer who, for a spell of something like a decade, lived in London, and for a briefer time within that something-like-a-decade, moved in the literary circles of East London, which is where I met him. In 2017 he disappeared, or jumped ship, cut and run? His writing had always raised a few eyebrows and so the joke the raised eyebrow wearers told was that he'd ended up in a psychiatric ward. I think he'd enjoy that. At any rate, social media averse Muller's trail runs dry across the Channel.

From the latter stages of his time in London, I acted as his editor, which isn't quite the right word for untangling his words, repurposing his "shoddy babble" as he called it. But I wasn't the only sucker performing that duty. There was another, the Poodle. Muller's brother, I think. And maybe another. It was unclear. Anyway, the something-like-a-decade Muller called London his home is captured within the stories that forge a novelette, here, in lieu of a memoir.

Inconsistencies kept in tact. I couldn't see how else to preserve... Tadhg.

— [Sean Preston], 2019.

Not long before he left London, he told me how he'd ended up here in the early 2000s. He said he'd actually left Tasmania for Afghanistan. In Kandahar, he'd "played a high value target in a game of chess, and won." By that point I'd learnt to smile politely and hope that I was supposed to be in on some sort of joke. I believed the Afghanistan bit, I think he'd convinced me as much previously in a conversation with more serious connotations, but the accompanying tales that followed just seemed too fantastical, too compelling, too convenient. I tried to suss him out, catch him in our own chess game, slowly picking off his pieces. I used this obvious chess metaphor, even, to make it clear that I was dubious. He laughed, "A dumb romantic to the last, he remained transfixed by the Queen, incapable of playing any other piece, unwilling to part with his muse. In chess, as in life, a fabricator, and a hopeless case."

This dream occurred at the dawn of the new millennium. I was twenty-one years old and had just arrived in Pakistan. That night I slept just across the border in no man's land, after travelling 10,000 kilometres overland on local transport from Cairo to "the Quetta I had to get to." The day before this dream, I'd made a rough and hasty exit from Iran, after staying there for a month, amidst much rambling. I left the Islamic Republic after difficulties with the police, as well as being tired of the relentless assault on my flesh by all the aged Persian queers thinking that I was a nice, fresh piece of arse just waiting to be fucked. I've tried to recreate the sense of this dream, which, technically, belongs to the sub-category of nightmare. I read somewhere once that twenty-five per cent of all dreams are nightmares, and that those who live in fear in their waking world are more likely to be gripped by the crippling effects of a nightmare. I don't swallow that. Most of my dreams, actually, fall into the sub-category of nightmare. Failing that, they are invariably erotica, of one form or another, but oddly enough, never of the furthermost sub-category: nightmare erotica. To be honest, I'm neither particularly fearful, nor particularly sexual. The frequency of my nightmares (and the erotica of my dreams) is, I think, just the way my brain digests the old diurnal grind, the uncooked meat of my reality. Finally, a confession: this dream possibly was fuelled by a month of *excess that was spent on a strict diet of high-grade Baluchi hash. And one more fact: the morning after this dream, I was asked to vacate the $1 a night hotel room that I was sleeping in. No explanations were given. I just headed for the train station. I kept on moving.*

I am in Quetta.

I am in Quetta.

In Quetta I am?

Am I in Quetta?

Is this Quetta I am in, is this the Quetta that I have to get to?

Beads running down my head and onto my pillow. It is sweat formed from my horror and helplessness, the helplessness that sits as a beast at the core of my dream.

Is this a room in Quetta? The room has a low roof pressing down, a room with windows, but no glass? There is no glass. A door, but no lock. Certainly, this is my room. And I can see movement. Cockroaches, insects (or is this really the room of insects?). The walls are a dark, dark green. I ask myself a crippling question: Is this the room? Is this the room, which I must get to?

From somewhere, in the depths of my sleep, I let out a cry. It is a cry on my first night in Pakistan.

I am in Quetta.

I am in Quetta.

In Quetta I am?

Am I in Quetta?

Is this Quetta I am in, is this the Quetta that I have to get to?

Faintly aware of noises, then of someone starting to shake me.
The anxiety of the waking world.

I am in Quetta.

How do I get to Quetta?

Will I get to Quetta!

[Tadhg! Tadhg! Tadhg!]

I have to get to Quetta?

How do I get to the place? I am in Quetta.

I must get to Quetta.

I must get into my room.

Tadhg! Tadhg! Tadhg!

And in this dream I suddenly have an urge to shatter everything, and I know I can't, that I cannot shatter this immaterial monstrosity, this haunted, shadowy feeling that is fleeing through me.

I have to get to Quetta

Am I awake?

Am I in the room?

Am I in Quetta?

Hands are shaking me now. I open my eyes, screaming, and I grip those hands with all my might, and without knowing why, I drag their nameless owner towards me, shouting, Who the fuck are you?

The reply is inaudible.

So I force the hands and the face forward toward me in the grubby dark, and I find myself staring right into the face of the hotel receptionist, the hotel receptionist of the cheapest hotel, in the town that I have come to, the town that is Quetta. My body is covered with sweat, and I am confronted by that glistening beast, my own nightmare, and I still cannot quite fathom if this is a dream, or if I have, in fact, returned to my hotel (the cheapest hotel in Quetta). Am I here? Is this a place that I have reached?

I fumble for a cigarette. The receptionist has left. My cigarette is a "47", a small Iranian smoke I had bought on what was yesterday in Zahedan. I light it up and study the room. The door has no lock. There is no light, and one window is smashed. I breathe the harsh nicotine and inhale, indulging the sense of something real, of something that can kill me. I look to the floor: my boots and my pack are where I left them - five tiles from the right, two tiles out. Nothing has been touched. I grab my torch, and my Don Quixote. I stay awake until the dawn. It is an unholy vigil, it is as though I am staying awake forever, waiting for the devil to come and take me.

The following was originally a standalone short story published in Open Pen Magazine, "In Lieu of a Memoir", from which this novelette takes its title. He read from it for us at the now defunct LXV Books in Bethnal Green. That was the first time I actually met him, but maybe the second or third time he'd met me, the bastard. He almost missed the event, he told some young drunks in The Florist pub after.

"I was so overwhelmed by the mass of people outside the bookshop when I arrived, I paused to consider my next move, thought about cutting and running," he confessed with tight-eyed gravity, "then a double-decker came, and the footpath cleared."

The bastard.

I'd wound up trudging through a bitter London winter in the guise of a would-be debt collector for an ailing bakery, run by an ex-model with a heavy cocaine habit, who was embarking on her first major literary work, "Lets Make Cupcakes, You and Me". I was working a seventy-hour week. After three months, the strain was telling. I'd grown detached from my wife, her frustration largely driven by my inability to provide sufficient means for our survival and by my shameless scrounging after other people's money. I'd been evicted from our flat and had taken to parking my sorry arse just about anywhere. In this condition of poverty, isolation and sexual frustration, I'd begun a romantic liaison with a Mongolian pâtissier, an illegal who'd trained in Novgorod, Russia, where she learnt to make the plumpest little pastries. We would fuck senselessly, with her long black hair falling loosely on the flattened bags of spilt flour which she lay on with her baker's apron rolled up to her tits and her legs spread apart, and me, awkwardly, with my boilers suit undone and tangled around my calves. We would finish and I would dust her generous hips and she would dust mine. There was no kissing, just fumbling and fucking, no goodbyes and no hellos. I'd go home empty and alone, my loins sucked dry, my battered little man incapable of pissing straight. The light would be out, a cold dinner would await me, and I'd hear the echoes of a line from some forgotten epic, recited to me back when the times were good, "He that eats alone, eats his own sins." In other words: eats shit!

And shit I ate. The work, the infidelity, the food without substance, the hustling. In the dark, I'd walk round my derelict West London flat like some hopeless soldier, like some would-be mercenary tucking my son in. I'd try to sleep but couldn't. Lying there, feeling dirty and ashamed, the only reprieve I could think of was to revive, once more, my stalled literary journey. I began to wonder: Were there other whores like me? Were there other artists who fucked tartars and who bummed other people's smokes, who scrounged around for money and put the heat on desperate men to pay the debts from which they were running? Poverty had made me cowardly. In my fear I'd become everything I hated. A drunk, a cheat, a womaniser, a liar, and a thief. So I decided to hunt down my lost companions, my literary posse. And that was how I initiated the so-called North North London Writers Group and began my own path toward redemption.

My inspiration, the North London Writers Group, I located late one night somewhere in cyberspace.

Immediately, when I opened up their website, it was as if I'd entered a room without windows, a room without doors. They declared they were "a friendly group of writers." I then read that not everyone could become a member. Their website said places were reserved for "journeymen with publication history" or for those now "seriously pursuing publication." "Journalists" and "MA graduates" could also be admitted. I had no publication history. I was not seriously pursuing publication. I was not a journalist, or an MA graduate. The bottom line was that this last ditch attempt at locating my own Jerusalem had ended in nothing but a fresh disappointment that I couldn't bear. And so began my electronic correspondence with that group, leading in turn to other electronic correspondence. It records a very awkward period in my life and so is repeated here in lieu of a memoir. And why not? After all, the conventions of memoirs have changed or should change. The true records of the day are incomplete and fleeting. No longer are they consigned to lost diaries and tattered note books, rather they will be found in the impulsive nattering, trails of cyber messages darting through light like misspent ejaculations.

Sent: 12 November 20XX 12:51 am
Subject: A Funeral Note

Hello Victor,
I am a unpublished writer, I am not a journalist, nor a MA graduate. I read the brief outline of your group and it read like an ad for a funeral in the Classifieds. the group sounds like a collection of evangelists, or fascists, or some queer incarnation of the two in literary form, perhaps even a selfhelp group for arseholes.
I think your membership should only include unpublished dropouts with current or former vices, little money, not much sophistication and serious time limitations. Perhaps they should even live in extreme circumstances that only allow them to write in the dark (much like the cave painters of old dripping blood on the walls). And what about single mothers with bold ambitions,

who put there children to bed, have a sniff of vix, and then write erotic novels, a paragraph a night, about literary groups in north London? That could be good. You could meet strictly at dawn? Anyhow, I have to write my six paragraphs, and rise at 5.15 am. Sadly for both of us i do not fit the criteria to join your group, much though I might benefit from it and even enjoy it.

I am thus considering starting the North North London Writers Group. It would be an alternative to the North London Writers Group. It would be based in the West, or the South, or the East, as the North is not on my radar and clearly its time to move. But, then, there is something to be said about the North North London Writers Group being somewhere other than the North.

Many thanks,

Tadhg Muller.

There was no reply. A small victory. With urgency, I set about sending the above message to a spiritual brother, a fellow dropout I'd befriended in a London kitchen, where we exchanged sordid anecdotes, usually about his escapades with Nothing Hill housewives, whilst he scrubbed dishes. He'd returned to Sydney to dig in and pursue his literary career as a crime novelist. As is the way, he was enjoying no success, but remained committed. I called him the Poodle, because his prose always spent too long in the salon. It never had a hair out of place. Perhaps that was the secret of his glorious, perpetual failure?

Sent: 13 November 20XX 8:40 pm
Fwd: A Funeral Note

Dear Poodle,
I started looking round, out of curiosity, for a writers group. God
knows why! Actually, its partly because I've decided that if we
leave this neighborhood and go either to the south or the east,
I'll try and start my own writers group. I think it will be effective,
as I am fairly good at that sort of thing - getting things started!!!
However, this triggered me to look at other writers group. I could
only find one called the North London Writers Group, I read the
criteria to join and realized that for me it was a none starter. So
I felt compelled to write them an email, entitled "A Funeral Note"
Having written this, and concluded that it was fairly ridiculous, I
realized the only person who would find it entertaining, with the
possible exception of Victor, is of course you.
Tadhg.

Sent: 14 November 20XX 12:45 pm
Re: Fwd: A Funeral Note

Tadhg,

I like it. I like it, and the funeral note. Sign me up.

The Poodle.

P.S. Could you send me the contacts for the North London Writers Group? I might email them suggesting a cultural exchange program with the Sydney Chapter of the North North London Writers Group.

Sent: 14 November 20XX 10.22 pm
Subject: Developments

Poodle,
This idea of the North North London Writers Co-op - I am not kidding. I really think I could be on to something. I am going to work on some ad's, start posting them across London with my son. I'll create contact details - an email adress - and send them to you. You can poster Sydney. Then, the North North London Writers Co-op can begin accepting submissions for its first publication of avant-garde writing entitled "Lost Chapters." Each member would submit one chapter, then we can select a number for publication in a cooperative novel, called "74 Hand Jobs" I'd present it to literary agents in London. As for the Co-op, there would be no rules except that before writing we'd have to swear a lot, and afterwards swagger a great deal. There would also have to be at least one sex scene every 6 pages, or perhaps every 6 minutes, as read by the semi- or sub-literate. I feel quite strongly about that. Any member who did not produce a sex scene often enough would have to be expelled. You could do likewise in Sydney – arrange some expulsions. I don't know about government funding but we

could only grow bigger, we could only grow stronger. God, we might even make a movie! There are no boundaries, my dear Poodle. There are only the stars!
Tadhg.

Sent: 16 November 20XX 12.42 pm
Re: Developments

Tadhg,

"There are no stars."
"I'll find them."

I owe you a serious email and one will come but not this afternoon, nor tomorrow, because I am getting out of here. This place really shits me. I am even beginning to sound like you.
As for the North North London Writers Group, I will only say this: we should always feel free to piss on one another, provided that the piss is a good piss, is a happy piss, and occurs outside in the open air, irrigating mutual thought under the stars. (Suggested new motto: "There are no stars." "I'll find them.")
In short, I remain,
Fraternally,
The Poodle of the North North London Writers Group
(But shouldn't it be a Collective?)

Sent: 16 November 20XX 12.01 pm
Subject: Bombard the Fuckers

Brother,

I am happy with the motto but would suggest another:

"I have been a con, it went wrong.
I was a fool, I learnt a lot."

I will get started on the posters.

Tadhg

P.S. The North London Writers Club hasn't responded. We shouldn't stomach that. I will get you their email address, when we're ready we will fucking strike - bombard the fuckers and tell them it's time they disolved, it's time they went back to journalism.

Sent: 18 November 20XX 1.45 am
Subject: North North London Writers Co-op

Poodle,

It's started: I posted a hand written sign outside Ladbroke Grove tube station at 5.45 am Saturday. It read:

 No Journalists

 No Postgraduates

 No White People

 The North North London Writer's Co-op

"There are no stars
And we'll find them."
- The Poodle (a founding member)
Fully independent writers group

Contact: Tadhg at
ThereRn0stars@gmail.com

Within a day there were three inquiries, one person became a member, another asked: Do you have a problem with white people? I answered that no man was white, the white man was a notion, the white man was the Diablo, incarnation of evil.

I didn't hear back.

Yours,
Tadhg

P.S. I am having a coffee with Lloyd Vigo next week, to talk about writing and to take the Group from two to three members (four if you include the Sydney branch).
P.P.S. According to my wife, my sign was gone by midday Saturday, which is a shame, as she did it, and, well, it looked pretty fucking hardcore.
P.P.P.S. "Bright, bright stars, baby, I can see them."

Sent: 21 November 2010 12.42 am
Re: North North London Writers Co-op

Tadhg,

Keep after the great white whale of the North North London Writers Group. There must be at least a short story there. You should write it in instalments (perhaps by email to a brother in Sydney who promises assistance but never delivers). By the way, that brother in Sydney has reservations about belonging to anything that is called a Co-op as opposed to a Collective. Because IN ANY MOVEMENT THERE MUST BE AT LEAST THE PROMISE OF VIOLENCE, and the term "Co-op" has, he thinks, unfortunate connotations of wholefoods restaurants in the seventies. Also, that brother in Sydney may be a wanker – indeed he recently posted signs around his desk saying I MUST NOT BE A WANKER – I repeat he may be a wanker, but still he believes the Collective's motto should take the form of a dialogue:

"There are no stars."

"I'll find them."

Which strikes, he thinks, the right note of intellectual courage in the face of grimly declared facts. Also (minor point) that brother would prefer that his name, even his pseudonym, weren't used anywhere, including on flyers in Ladbroke Grove. Why? Just because it's his name, I suppose, and he will attach what statements he wishes to it. Use your own name, or your own nom de guerre, if you have to.

I remain with goodwill,
The (Existential) Poodle.

Sent: 21 November 2010 2.30 am
Subject:

I am writing the short story. It is entitled: "Not in my brother's name."
Tadhg.

Sent: 25 November 2010 12.42 am
Subject:

Tadhg,

I intend to dedicate my crime novel, titled"Murder 74", to the North North London Writers' Group.
Yours,
The Poodle
P.S. "Murder 74" is set in a retirement village just outside Sydney.

Sent: 25 November 2010 8.45 pm
Subject: News from the Fat Badger

Poodle,
i met Lloyd Vigo at the Fat Badger. He asked me where

the rest of the group was? I say "I'm it," and he asks me whether I'm "having a laugh." I tell him I'm not a fucking

comedian. He says he's written three sci/fi novels:

1. *The Doom*
2. *Lost in Constellation 26*, and:
3. *No War Without Charlie*

I say I like the titles. He goes "I brought you a chapter" I take a look at the first paragraph and tell him it's hilarious, and he asks me once more if I'm having a laugh I tell him again that I'm not a comedian. He says WHERE is everybody else? And I repeat "I am it, Lloyd" Then the whole thing started to get a messy edge, just a bad fucking air. He asks me what have I got to show for it? I say "Just the odd chapter and some note books" He says again: "Are you having a laugh?" For the third time I repeat I am not a comedian and I tell him that the meeting is becoming tiresome. He says "Yes, this is a waste of time you're obviously a fraud." I tell him I know a good literary group he could join. It's called the North London Writers Group. He says: Hang on isn't that us? I tell him to watch it(!) this is the North North London Writers Co-op and he better watch his mouth when it comes to the North London Writers Group. The man has the nerve to ask me yet again whether I'm having a laugh. I tell him he'd better clear out, because quite frankly he's not the kind of person that we're after in the North North London Writers Co-op.

Tadhg.

Sent: 30 November 2010 12.43 pm
Re: News from the Fat Badger.

It has the appearance of the real!
The Poodle

Sent: 30 December 2010 4.30 am.
Subject: More from the Fat Badger

Poodle,
I just met Tom Morgan, 19. He saw the ad at Ladbroke Grove tube station and took a month to follow up. Nice guy, we met at the Fat Badger. Then he asked about the quote on the sign from the Poodle, he said he liked the quote. He asked me what else I could tell him about the Poodle? I told him all I could say is that the Poodle was part of the sydney wing though there is already a schizm. The Poodle was with the Collective and we were the co-op. then he asks whether i have any of your writing and I say I'm not at liberty to say. The Poodle is the real thing a kind of one man secret society and well he gets angry if anyone speaks for him, if anyone makes statements in his name. So I couldn't say anything except that the Poodle spent some time in the service. He asks if I mean military then says "Afghanistan?" and I tell him not to be so pushy though I knew you'd once travelled over the Karakorum. He asked "Where the fuck is that?" and I say "Tribal areas of Pakistan" It went well after that. Tom drank a few pints, then pulled out a joint

and suggested we go for a walk.

Poodle...... you already have a cult following and there is a rumour in the London literary underground that you were once a spook running operations across the Afghan border.

Tadhg.

Sent: 1 January 2011 12.25 pm
Subject: Happy New Year

Tadhgy,

I have a poem for you to give to Tom. It begins: "I cannot love you." Maybe you should recite it together at the next meeting of the Co-op?

Yours,

The Poodle.

Sydney

"Sire not children by a woman who wears gold jewellery," Pythagoras

I cannot love you

the rigor mortis of your smile is a woman with a price on her

head and eyes like cash registers

your lies, your lies, and the bullshit that follows your skin-deep

optimism

I am heading south

here the sky's great vacancy is a mouth or an arsehole admiring itself:
nothing but borrowed phrases and slogans in lieu of thought
your ladies of fashion I cannot tell from the creatures of the
night

So this is my goodbye

At dawn the cathedral I love sails up College Street like a ghost ship

But you I cannot love
and the men, Staffordshire terriers, wear their flesh like jewellery,
or armour, or jewellery and armour, that late imperial style!
Sydney your face is fat, it is fat your face, and
pampered, without definition

I am heading south
You are a simian circus a screen of anxiety There is no victory here
in the war on excrement

You are slimy as an overripe mango. You are oily as cockroach shit You are
a total moral and physical dump. Sydney

This is my goodbye.

Sent: 1 January 2011 3.14 am
Re: Happy New Year

You miserable cunt, We do not respond to poetry submissions.

Sent: 17 January 2011 2.35 am
Subject:

Poodle,
tomorrow I have a meeting with Joe Fagottini, he deals in little bundles of romance, and has a sideline in ripped-off cook books. Tom's coming too. Then we're all going to drift up to the north, cruise around. Tom thinks Islington is the best bet. We'll look for a pack of wankers flicking over their pages, then we're going to try and beat the shit out of them, let them know whats what. Let those bastards know that this is serious, that they are rude fuckers for not getting back to me, those fuckers in the North London writers group.
I'm tired brother. More fucking snow more fucking rice and pasta, more spartan living. I need some warm clothes.
Tadhg

Sent: 18 January 2011 12.36 pm
Re:

Jo Fagottini? Did you fabricate all of this? I don't mind, but I'm at the point where, henceforth, my dealings with you will be

conducted via my secretary. His name is Ernst Wanke.
The Poodle

Sent: 18 January 2011 10.17 pm
Re: Re:

Poodle,
Like all history, some of it happened, some of it didn't. What
mattered was what was born, what came from it: the North
North London Writers Collective.

Tadhg

Sent: 21 January 2011 12.22 pm
Re: Re: Re:

Don't be slippery. Did any of this take place? Are you still in
London?

Sent: 21 January 2011 1.25 am
Subject: Confessions of a Drunk, a Cheat, a Womanizer,
a Liar and a Thief

The meeting with Lloyd took place. Unfortunately, that was it.
There was no more interest. As I told you, the sign didn't last
long on Ladbroke Grove.
Tadhg.

Sent: 22 January 2011 12.17 am
Re: Confessions of a Drunk, a Cheat, a Womanizer, a Liar and a Thief

You are, in fact, a bastard.

The next morning I rocked up at the bakery at a quarter to six, still high on the dreams of my encounters with that imaginary body of writers, the North North London Writers Group, a set of encounters that, I realised, had just come to an end. But, walking the streets, I couldn't escape the feeling that my world, having gone from bad to worse, and then worse again, was about to change once more, and incontrovertibly. Yes, it was as if, through my fabrications, I'd shaken off all the cowardice, all the fear, the worthlessness and isolation, that had dragged winter into the pit of my soul. I found my boss in her office. She was at her desk, typing away at the final draft of *"Let's Make Cookies, You and Me."* She was working hard to meet the deadline imposed by insatiable penguins. Her radio was blaring Travie McCoy 'Billionaire'. I picked up a page.
Still working on this crap? I said.
She sat back obviously stunned, obviously wounded, but mostly just aware of the truth of my statement.
You're fired, Tadhg.
I nodded and thanked her and so walked out, past the Tartar who offered me one last smile, then closed the door on that world, a world that was a far greater lie than all the fictions I'd

concocted. I didn't know where I was going. It was minus two degrees outside, the air was a bitter cocktail of ice and snow. Yet, inside me, I felt that I was done with being everything I hated. I knew that I was set upon being the person I really was – whatever that is; literature and the power of words? – at any rate, myself. Or as the Poodle had it:

"There are no stars."
"I'll find them."

To try and give you an idea of how Tadhg was viewed, I was once asked, "Tadhg Muller, dissident Republican or Nazi?"

"What bastard," he said, when I fancied winding him up, "said that? The spoken word poet speaking poems with his mouth full of pies? The elongated Scotsman? The bear-Woolf? The Brick Lane bookseller? A SHON!? The one obsessed with elephants? I forgive them. Just tell me it wasn't the Irish porn star."

Muller detested the latter writer, I never asked why. But his relationship with writers, writing, fiction, art, always felt prickly in a way that not only presented in Tadhg, but also anyone in his company.

He wasn't a magnetic type, as others had it. He was just contagious. I didn't respond, so he sent me the following:

I struggled to establish my credentials as a dropout. In London, I made a first-rate error. Starting out in West London, I worked the fashionable joints in that human wasteland, that feeding ground for The Big Game, capital of dead souls. Clearing tables, stacking shelves, cutting Roquefort, hand carving Iberico de Bellota, handing out Parisian sticks, lobes of Foie Gras Entier, etc, etc. Day jobs gorging the fat creatures of West London: arms dealers, bankers, actors, the old money, the new money, Tories wearing blue, Tories wearing yellow, Saudi princes, aristocrats, royals, oligarchs, every conceivable incarnation of shitface you could imagine, patrons of the arts. A demographic glimpse from the other side of a counter, from the other end of a blade, behind menu or table, from over above a La Marzocco with a perfect shot extracting, like the tail of a mouse, and me looking out at the world.

As a friend, a KP (kitchen porter) from Krakow liked to say (when he stumbled up from a subterranean kitchen infested with rats... for a drink... and some fresh air):

Here come tit and arse painter... there go Saudi arms dealer... and godfather of reality TV... the beneficiary of Russia's shift to private ownership... they go around, and around... coffee for the head of IMF... there go the vastards... looks at them... vat, ugly vuckin vastards ... Tadhg stop looking! Espresso, two sugar, snap! snap!

That part of town represented our hereditary disease: the West.

A sick old man that people like to toast.

I'd often make my way away from it, south of the Thames, why not? On one such trip I found myself at a crow's bookshop near the dinosaur park, eyes falling upon a face, a set of eyes belonging to the preeminent British painter Leonard Fuhriman on the cover of the latest chapter of his deification amongst the London cultural establishment, 'Breakfast with Leonard'. Looking into the cover, those eyes, I recalled my meeting with the painter on a distant morning, having fallen out of one bad job and slap bang into another. Working behind the counter of one of Mr. Fuhruman's stops. The staff viewed his daily arrival as a perk of the job. They could see the famed artist, bring him his weak coffee, and after a time exchange remarks, be sunned by his eccentricity.

A local girl and I had started there at roughly the same time, and we stood behind the counter as he strode in, not missing much with his strange eyes. He was old, bent, and craggily faced, with those eyes wide open, open as if he had a matchstick jammed between each lid. The image of the artist, straight from a postcard, coated in paint, dishevelled, sharp, gaunt, concentrated, intense. He walked in with a jolt, the old fuck, picked up a bar of nougat and tossed it, up into a bow trajectory, over at the new girl. An act to be considered as further confirmation of his peculiar genius, as confirmation of his disregard for convention. The girl, to script, stumbled and just about caught it, blushing crimson. The next day it was my turn. As this clockwork fraud arrived, I looked around and to my satisfaction realised it was just the two of us. I had thought on the previous event, the act of Leonard throwing the bar of nougat, of the girl stumbling, and him paying, and the action explained by the fact that he was a rare genius - not a stupid fucking prick. And the girl, she was lucky, the girl, she had had the privilege of catching his genius. When Leonard walked in that second time I concluded that I would not fall victim to his stupid fucking genius.

I took it in the left hand, mid-air, nice and high. In Tasmania we play bloody good cricket, we breathe this shit.

I remember having read somewhere how the great artist liked horses. It made sense.

He paused, and turned his head to take a better look at me, opened his eyes wide, very wide, wider than usual. He'd realised I'd anticipated his behaviour. He realised he'd been anticipated.

And now looking at his face on a book cover in South London it was clear that he was the perfect artist, and now the perfect corpse, for this dumb age.

Still, my first instinct writing this is that an attack on the dead, even one so slight, seems wrong. But Fuhriman represents more than his work. He represented, and captured, the heart of the established order and its celebration, all those lords and ladies of art, and all that pedigree, including the shit and shitfaces he painted.

He is of the world of a half baked genius in a world run by and made for other half baked fools.

In a new now, now, sometime later, from the other side of a menu, a table, a counter, a whatever, I conclude: there is a time for dancing on the graves of the dead, and shit, the time is now. All those bastards from another time, to hell with them.

And so these fictions he put out in various magazines, these short stories, autofictions, gonzo memoirs, that were sometimes *not* in magazines, but in my inbox at 4am, I think, painted their own portrait of Tadhg Muller, amidst his tenure as a Londoner, as an artist.

People like to chat shit. And Tadhg was often the shit they liked to chat about. They'd say nasty stuff that I'd laugh at, like: "He works in an office."

But I knew he was a wine man by trade. And cheese. A food buyer of some sort. That's why he's ended up in mainland Europe, I think. But they said worse, that he never penned a single story. They were the work of his brother, a disturbed individual, or maybe even me or new boy. Idiots.

Either way, Tadhg Muller was a sort of fiction, they said. No wife, no kids. Just a lonely Tasmanian writing from his locked room, posting stories to and as "Tadhg".

It was dark by the time he started down the road, a suitcase once again by his side, a small satchel over his shoulder that contained a giant outdated laptop. He headed in the direction of a friend, a very old friend. It wasn't much of a walk from one end of Notting Hill to the other, the Harrow Road to the far side of Ladbroke Grove, under the west way and up the hill. The sun had fallen behind the terraces that climbed like the heads of organ pipes, a metaphor he would often repeat in the clubs and bars of the neighbourhood, one he stole from the mountain vista of his childhood. The headlights of cars coming down from Notting Hill Gate greeted his ascension. Through a gate, overgrown with roses, and at the door, warn and tired, he paused. Before he knocked, he took a moment to compose himself, to adjust his shirt, pull a comb, and very firmly reestablish the parting on the left side of his head.

He tapped gently on a wrought iron knocker, and the nervous rapping of the cold metal elicited no response from within, just the hollow echo of its own question. He knocked harder, and then obstinately harder. Nothing. The wind picked up, and with it he shivered a little, someone had walked upon his grave. Rose was out, then. He set his suitcase down, and decided to stay and wait under the veranda on the first floor, the main entry to the old terrace mansion, a place now squalid and decrepit, at odds with the rest of the street, with their private gardens and European sports cars. He sat down, realising that he was tired. Another small shiver. *I am tired, tired and cold. I am tired, tired and cold.* His eyes grew heavy, perhaps it was those eyelids that played tricks with his mind, maybe he was dreaming - Snap out of it, Tadhg - he snapped out of it, out of sleep, studied the dark before him. The first sign of rain illuminated in the orbs of light from street lamps. Finally the gate opened. Two policemen entered, no greetings, just a few brief questions, some phone calls, and the frustrated realisation that the young man was doing nothing wrong, just soberly waiting on the steps of a friend's house on a cold and miserable winter's night with a suitcase, waiting quite calmly without menace, just his own frustration. One cop offered a cigarette, shook his head muttering about neighbours, and the two swung the gate shut, and then they were gone.

That's when the rain really got going. It wouldn't have been much if it wasn't for the wind which brought the rain in from both sides under the veranda. It began to lash and chop, and what foliage was left on the skeletal limbs of the Autumn trees began to give in to the wind's embrace, to dance, cheek to cheek, but never landing, never stopping.

He said something to himself.

The door to Rose's basement flat opened, but a fearful looking fellow appeared, handsome eyes watching from behind round spectacles, spectacles that slid momentarily down his long aquiline nose, to be returned to its rightful place by an elegant finger, the finger of a pianist.

Inside the warmth of the house, the rambler sat down on the sofa, and looking at his guest sat the lodger on a cushion. Aziz was his name, and Aziz was Iranian, one of Rose's lodgers from the city that was half the world: Esfahan. Rose's collection of weirdos, artists, social freaks, PHD students, composers, writers, painters, bums, were the delicate souls that made Rose's grasp and possession of the Notting Hill terrace mansion possible. How beautiful a colour were Aziz's eyes, green Chinese stones, polished till they resembled the eyes of a purring cat that had just caught her supper. They darted left and right, as Aziz turned from the window and back to his guest excitedly, or distractedly turned to his silent television screening Sochi, the Winter Olympics, nothing that mattered, nothing that was very important.

Aziz had questions for him. Was he expected? Would this be a problem? Who was he? Was he a friend? Did he know Rose wasn't normally out this late? There was a planning meeting that concerned changes to the access of the communal garden, and this was very important. Something about London clay, hard clay. Aziz was a sculptor, another artist. Aziz rubbed his hand across his flat belly and smiled, his eyes squinting with the smile's force. The conversation turned to the monotony of work and the guest remained tactfully silent. let Aziz talk about his cake business - tortes,

cheesecakes, tea breads, Bakewells, the dull monotony of
the grind, this they both understood and so they laughed.
Aziz offered his guest a rum, his eyes steadier and steadier,
the man himself became more and more comfortable, and
the room grew warmer as if a wood fire had begun to burn.
It must have been getting late. The rain had stopped. They
discussed Iran, the Pope and the Church, English gardens,
the Monarchy, President Putin and Pussy Riot. The guest
pulled a cigarette and lit up with dexterity. Aziz, through
a puff of blue smoke, rushed to the window, animatedly,
and opened it with a laugh saying something halfheartedly
about the sensitivity of the decor. The stranger decided
to go outside and to smoke the cigarette in peace. When
he returned, Aziz had taken off his shoes and was lying
on the sofa. The stranger enquired whether there wasn't
something that he could be doing, and Aziz replied that it
wasn't often that he had guests. The stranger in turn said
that he wasn't strictly speaking a "guest", and that he was
in fact a stranger. Aziz, smiling, said that the man did not
seem like a stranger, commented on his eyes, how they were
a strange colour, how they were perhaps born from blue,
but more grey, ashen grey like a worn Baluchi carpet. And
Aziz rolled a joint with a little hash and asked if together
perhaps they might smoke it. The ill effects of smoke
were forgotten. It was good, Aziz said. They relaxed, now,
Aziz on the sofa, his delicate soft hands inside his shirt,
his elegant fingers   caressing his lower stomach muscles,

flat and ripped. And Aziz was asking about the guest's sexuality, if he had ever been with a man. He told him that he was with a man, lent forward and, pausing, studied the guest's face, hungry eyes, no longer beady but rounded out, full, famished. Aziz removed his shirt, the heat of the room more evident now, and showed his smooth athletic torso. The stranger sat up staring across the great expanse of the drug-fucked and fogged room into his those green eyes.

And Aziz said if the stranger might like to be with him, it would please Aziz. And for a moment the stranger paused. Aziz, sensing his vulnerability, began to tell a story of when he did military service in Iran, how he had been at a station on the border, how it was an isolated border. And how one night a soldier had asked him the same question, and he thought this wrong, but the soldier told him that he could, that he could do it, that he would enjoy it. And they lay down next to each other and he put his erect penis into the other man, and the man had told him that he was happy when he felt the moisture inside him, he knew Aziz was happy. And the stranger thanked him for the story, and Aziz asked if he understood the story. And the stranger realised that he had stopped looking for Rose and wondered how he had ended up in this room with the Iranian. And Aziz turned and stretched out on the sofa looking to the stranger, and then he, the stranger, walked towards him and picked up the tin of hash and rolled a smoke, collected his bag and went to wait at the front door, involuntarily, a programmed response.

And there he was once again outside the door. The wind blowing and the tricks of the night. The police? No, not a shadow. But the police might return. And complicate things. And the rain, falling as the light was falling, falling from the street lamps that were suspended with the other lights, a row of suns. *The hash is having an effect*. The hash was having an effect, he reflected. The stranger considered, yes, the police might return and do him for some minor drug offence. He looked back at the basement flat, Aziz looking out of the the window at him. He realised he had left something in there. His small satchel that he'd worn over his shoulder that contained a giant outdated laptop. He wouldn't wish to loose or misplace an idea, not when time was short. The rain fell harder. The stranger turned back and walked down the stairs and into the flat. Once more they both sat down, this time on the sofa. And the room was warm. And somewhere, surely now, a fire was burning, a faint flame, some smoke and coals, coals glowing, bright like Aziz. They shared a glass of Rum. The drink was warm, syrupy with a note of honey. It wasn't bad. He looked at Aziz, who was touching his chest, taking the stranger in once more. The spinning was room, and the lashing was rain, lashing against the window with great fury, and the smoke, and the eyes, and the rum, the stranger back lay. He felt his own arousal, his exhaustion, and the fear of his weight that hung eyes on his heavy, and a feeling, another feeling that seemed to grow him inside deep. Aziz, very gently and very tenderly, lent his hand to the stranger's trousers, and the stranger reclined as if he was inside sleep, felt the softness of Aziz's ripe mouth surround him. *Is this a dream?* and he wondered for a moment, was this a dream? Was this a prelude to some nocturnal emission? The stranger arched back, and opened his eyes to see Aziz kneeling down with his penis still inside his mouth. The fear of weight eyes from his lifted. The stood stranger, Aziz backed look.

I thought he'd ended up in Europe because someone told me that they'd seen him in Paris, in La Belle, France, where he had started defacing National Front posters, his eldest holding the tape. He took fatherhood, and his children's education, very seriously.

I asked to talk to Portugo.

The word was out that he was done, the word was out that he would soon get the chop. Perhaps I felt some responsibility, after all I'd discouraged him from taking that job driving a bus. I'd told him he'd lose his mind. He'd already lost it anyway. But still, I'd persisted and fought my corner, and lined up a promotion that would keep Portugo in the business, and he stayed, that was before things started crumbling and everything went to hell. An immigrant's hell. Feeling the heat. Having a bird and a child. Heat at work, heat on the job, feeling it burn down on his neck, hotter than the Lisbon sun. Then I'd been taken aside and asked by the boss: *What's happened to Portugo?* She'd told me it wasn't working with him, and once more I found myself fighting his corner, even though somewhere along the line we too had fallen foul of one another, and somehow things between us had rotted in the heat. Portugo, with his newly found authority had taken to bullying the workers. They'd once been my workers. Turned me cold on him, knowing he was digging his own grave. That was wrong. I was wrong. I should never have done that for him... to him. But I wouldn't let them throw the earth on him. I asked the boss if I could try and talk to him.

There I was, outside his apartment door, Portugo's new place, just above the shop - he'd split from the missus, she'd taken the kid. The door looked thin, and the walls of the hall were plastered brazenly across the countless cracks.

Portugo!

Portugo, why didn't you stay at home?

Portugo had said it was worse there.

Worse than what?

Than things falling to pieces?

I wondered for a minute if I was somehow to blame. Would he have been better driving a bus? I pictured him with his dull energy and pride, those intelligent eyes, and that sharp tongue running loose on London's streets, in some catastrophe like a traffic jam, cursing the day he'd been born, cursing the day he grew poor, the day the world had gone mad, cursing this place he'd been born into.

Portugo!

And then I knocked on the door.

And he let me in and I looked round.

And twelve months ago he came to London with his family. He came from Lisbon, from a slum end of that city, a city in a country crippled twice over. Portugo hadn't come with much, and he hadn't left much behind. Once more, his room was empty, even what family he had was gone.

On the table there was a six-pack of Portuguese beer, Sagres, and a blood sausage that would best be eaten cooked. Portugo had turned the drink and the sausage out in hospitality, testament to his decency.

We sat down.

He thanked me for coming, acknowledged in straightforward terms that even though I was a bastard, I hadn't give up on him, and that I was there to talk. I said that this was true, to talk, and with a smile he intimated that perhaps that meant I was not a bastard anymore. A liar and a schemer perhaps, but not a bastard. And with a smile of my own I said we could talk work, but not for long, we could talk work for ten minutes, and then all that would be left to talk about was life.

So Portugo knew he'd keep his job, messengers like me aren't sent to people that don't keep their job, those messages, after all, are delivered by another kind - human resources officers who trade in human stock. And fight though we had, and even hate each other as it had seemed, Portugo knew that I liked him, and that, with my stupidity being what it was, I would fight his corner, even if this would cause me problems and cost me a few hard months. I was selfish like that.

All this Portugo knew, and so our business talk was brief and he thanked me for delivering the message, and taking the time.

And tilting my drink I thanked him for the second beer and asked if I might have one of his cigarettes?

We'd already had a go at the blood sausage (which both of us concluded would best be eaten cooked and seasoned) and very gratefully I took one of Portugo's smokes, hoping I might incinerate the taste of the sausage with the tang of a harsh smoke.

On standing up, now that the business was over, and breathing the smoke in, I paused to enjoy the inhaling and the exhaling, as if this were some form of meditation, and, as I did so, very slowly, I looked around the room and I breathed it in too.

I looked at Portugo. Short, solid form, the strong line of his jaw, yes, a handsome face, the deep set brown eyes, the well groomed and proud air of a Mediterranean man, and then the smartness of his eyes and their stillness, suggesting a freedom from agitation my own character could never attain.

That empty room. Empty, save for a chair, a television, some plates, a kettle, a bookshelf. And there on the bookshelf a book, the book I'd given him, a Bukowski number. I smiled and thought Bukowski would've been happy to have been there, the only book on that sad empty bookshelf.

And I looked once more at Portugo, Portugo stubborn as an ox, who wasn't going to break or kick over for anyone.

Bukowski would be glad to be here, I remarked.

And he laughed, and picking up the book, he flicked through it.

Don't know if I'd be glad to have him here, one of us would have to go, he boasted.

Portugo, there's not much here, I concluded.

Portugo agreed, and, standing like me, cracked open a third beer with a coin and passed it my way, opened the cap of his own bottle, tossed the cap and the coin, and we tapped bottles and smoked a second cigarette, and Portugo paused, leant over to the shelf, picked up a box.

Let me show you something, he said.

There he was as a boy in Portugal in a faded photograph, in a shot with his mother and father.

My father was a drunk.

I nodded and looked at the picture.

Violence was part of every home, he said, and I signalled my understanding of this alien sentiment. *We got on well,* and then I saw his face cloud over, and grow dark, and he looked meaningfully at the face in the picture, a face markedly different to his own.

I was in Porto when one of my father's friends told me he'd died. He had drunk himself to the ground, and when they found him he had this in his pocket, his friend kept it for me.

Heavily, as if this was part of the burden that had a hold on him, Portugo pulled from the box a crumbled paper packet of cigarettes, bent and creased with the clutches of a hand letting go of life.

Is there anything in it? I asked.

Portugo looked at me, really took me in, and I could see that his face was tired, that he was worn, alone, and most of all that he was young.

A last cigarette, he replied, seriously, as if this was the most precious thing on the earth.

I asked myself what kind of hell is this, what kind of

world that the poor are condemned to, holding on to, and clutching empty treasures, and not knowing why. I shook my head, something building in me like rage. I tell him:

You ought to smoke that cigarette and be done with it.

I can't, replied Portugo, regret in his voice.

I picked up the matches, my eyes locked on Portugo, and, for a moment, it was as if the two of us filled that empty room.

Portugo, go on. Do it. Smoke that thing and be done with it.

But he just looked at me silently, looked me square in the eyes as if I had threatened or challenged him, and those other features unique to his face and his character take hold, those features firmly embedded in Portugo.

You ought to smoke it and be done with it, I said, softly this time.

Portugo's face softened. With paternal care, as if he might have woken it, he returned the last cigarette to that crumpled pack, and the crumpled pack to the box, and the box, with the last cigarette, sits, once more, on the empty shelf, beside Charles Bukowski.

Muller had let me know about about an old, fairly famous literary figure he'd befriended. Wise to the Tasmanian's game by now, I entertained him much in the way the Poodle had previously. Couple of pinches of salt. So when, at a book launch in Soho, Muller turned up in a black cab and helped the elderly author in question out of the vehicle, I let out a laugh at myself.

Some kinda man.

It was hot, and I could have done with a drink.

I checked my phone and caught the time, thought better of stopping. No, I'd make my way. So it was up the road, a scribbled address on a torn piece of paper in my hand. Still I couldn't help but think that this wasn't right, that I'd come the wrong way. God knows why. God and the Devil and my instincts. I remembered something about the man's friend from the previous night. His pained instructions to the taxi driver about the address, a possible mistake with the postcode, the need to drive with caution, as if the taxi driver and the artist were journeying through the Congo, not a little way across London.

The more I looked, the more my instincts were confirmed. They'd both talked of a block of flats as if they were sordid tenements. All I could see were nice houses, more European luxury cars parked outside. Not my end of town, anymore.

My grotto, he'd called it, in that clever, husky voice the previous night.

And now nothing around here looked like a block of flats, just a street full of boutiques.

I typed the address in my phone without the postcode, and came up with three possibilities, one in Colorado, one in Toronto and the third in London. I crushed the piece of paper again and shoved it in my pocket.

I wanted to be done with this. I just wanted to be done with it.

I took up the iPhone and rang and he picked up the phone. Old and raspy he sounded. As if he was on the other side of oblivion. Asking: Where was I? Why had I gone to that goddamn station! Was I crazy! I would walk? Walk? It would take an age, surely I could just get a taxi? No I couldn't, I told him. I didn't have the money. Do as you like, do as you like. And I said, no problem, no problem (as if I was saying: go fuck yourself). I figured it would take me ten and told him so. He doubted that. Fuck you, you bastard! Even though you're old - yes - even though you're old I'll still respect you and give no quarter. So fuck you, fuck you to oblivion! I'm goddamn coming!

It wasn't difficult to find the door. Perhaps the old man had concluded, on the previous night, that I was like the bulk of my generation - an idiot. I remembered reading somewhere that he'd had seven wives and fifteen children. Hell, what did that matter? I had one. Maybe if I made it to such a ripe old age I'd have had half a dozen more? I doubted it. The flesh had never meant that much to me.

The door was open. And I was greeted with a vision of the old man, a slice through the hall.

There he was seated on his deck. Crooked. Like a tree on a barren hill in winter, a tree that stands naked and all that's left of it, its gnarl, its harsh lines, its stressed limbs, clawing to the earth, driving its roots down through the soil, through the stone, clawing, clawing, clawing, despite the abandonment, the desolation, the wretchedness and the wind and the winter, the grim, bitter, bloody, violent earth.

His bony painter's hand, like the sharp talons of a raptor, was holding a long brush very calmly, seriously, deliberately. It was in stark contrast to the character that had held court last night at the exhibition opening, amongst that crowd of young artists and dealers. I couldn't see the image below his hand. It was obscured from my gaze, his body frozen in the peaceful execution of his craft.

I don't know how long I watched the old man, his hair thick and matted, his old shirt torn on the shoulder, and his old track pants, his bare feet. I could see his calves, heavy and soft with age, like slow cooked meat waiting to fall from the bone.

The room was spare, orderly. It wasn't his home. I imagined his place in Marseille - somehow quite different, brighter, with its paintings, and books, and statues. I'd seen an old article in *The Times* which mentioned the splendour of that home.

There was smoke in the room, emanating from a cigarette in an ashtray behind him. Heavy black smoke. A strong cigarette. I knocked. He turned, looking far more vital than the man I'd studied the previous night. He picked his smoke up, raised it to his dry lips and then pulled it away to rest above his knee, a long piece of ash held there.

Well! Come in, he said, and exhaled a smoke ring, and the smoke and words came across the room, and I drew them in. I felt tired then, quite suddenly. In a world that by and large was headed slowly towards the grave, where in the end one was left with the choice of feeling tired or feeling miserable, it was a good thing to feel tired.

Well? he repeated. *Come in.*

His tone was grand, regal, aloof. It said that whatever all this is, this world and this life, I am above it, I am done. Something inside me said this was the way he'd always been, now and through to eternity.

I stepped into the room and returned the spectacles and the photographic images that he'd left at the opening.

He didn't ask about the show and I had nothing to say. I looked around the room, as if seeking an exit.

The old painter raised his voice slowly, in a barbed tone:

Well, is that it? Your curiosity satisfied?

There was scorn in the challenge but it felt hollow and deep inside his question you could hear the ring of frustration. I looked into his old eyes, and he looked back at me. I turned and, finding a chair, sat myself down, uninvited. I was hot, and I was tired, and I would sit.

My curiosity satisfied? I paused, as though I was mulling it over. *Yes*, I answered.

Well, you were quick, he remarked. *Coffee? I promised you a coffee. Good coffee. Illy,* he continued, then stood up, and hobbled into the adjoining kitchenette where he struggled with the machine, struggled to turn the handle to extract the coffee, remarking indifferently about how he'd never been mechanical. What was the need?

A thoughtful pause, and a yank, and the coffee was in.

And more remarks about London and his bloody kids. None of them understood, none were artists. Another pause as he turned and studied me:

You did well from me!

I didn't respond.

Sugar? he asked, as if to say, well come on, you did, didn't you?

And it was true I had done well, I had milked his name for all it was worth. And even now it didn't mean or matter that much to me.

Two, I answered. *Well stirred.*

He stirred three large sugars into the espresso, and brushed a lock of hair from his face.

Where was I? he continued, absently. Yes, his estate, his body of work, the major pieces. A series from the sixties, in particular when he was at his height, pieces that had never been shown, how could they? Such a large body of work, such a major contributor. These were the pieces that now troubled him, this was the dilemma that occupied his mind and prevented him from further work. His friend, the other artist, who'd come last night, he'd be executor of the estate. He had seen what children could do - other people's children. It wasn't that he didn't trust his. He'd just seen what people's children could do.

Were any of them artists? I asked.

No, none.

My father was a doctor and none of us were doctors.

An eyebrow raised. And then he opened his mouth, just slightly, a smoke held between his prominent long teeth.

You know on my mother's side I am a prince, he said.

I nodded absently, thinking that on my mother's side I am a madman.

But a doctor... and well, your last name, Muller. Like mine, Swiss.

And I told him the story of my grandfather.

When I finished, the old man opened his eyes, they had been closed for a time, as if at some point he'd stopped listening, remained fixed on one part of my story. Where in Africa had I said my grandfather had been?

Nigeria.

When?

The thirties.

And the old artist sighed. *My father was in Africa in the thirties selling engineering equipment. They probably knew each other. What was the name of the company?*

It was a Swiss company. I don't know the name.

And then he asked me if I was Roman Catholic. I answered in the affirmative. And surely, surely I, too, had been educated by the Jesuits? *No.* Surely not the Christian brothers? He wouldn't have it, the Jesuits had left their mark on me! Perhaps my father, I mused.

I think I've got you worked out, he remarked. *I admire you, yes. Though I have you worked out, and I see you've drunk your coffee. That was fast. How was it?*

A little thin, I said.

You son of a bitch, he replied. *If you wanted something different you should have asked for it. A ristretto!*

This time I paused. He was an interesting man. Spindly, and still a long, long way from giving in, from rolling over and dying. Death would have to take him by siege. Death would have to dig under his towers and bomb his walls. Death would need to starve him of supplies. Death would have to hunt him day and night, until this man, finally, was submerged by the sea. He neither deserved nor required my pity, good manners or gratitude. I would be pleased to leave, to return to my own painting. I would be pleased to leave him alone.

I could see his face begin to turn. a cloud above him, irritated, mostly at my presence. Yes, a look of irritation.

He drew the cigarette back to his lips, leant back. I knew it was time to go, time to go, get away from this thing crowding in on me. This thing, and this old man I admired greatly.

Thanks for returning my things... Time you got out of here!

Like a sledgehammer. And more than that blunt force, he was saying, what the hell are you wasting your time here for? Go out there and do it.

I think it is, I replied.

I got up and went to the door not looking back and headed into anonymity, swept back into the crowd, the crowd that made me weak, feeble, ashamed. Once more I wanted to be alone. Once more it was time to vanish.

And damn this city. Damn all islands.

Muller had cut his hair very short, I noticed, in the Red Lion near Elephant and Castle. He told me that he had given up writing for a trial spell. At night, he'd been walking the Thames instead. I laughed at that. Out in the rain on one such walk, he continued, he had become a boy, his younger self, and in the shade of St. Kats he saw a long-dead writer, who he wouldn't name, only to say that it was an author who never set foot in London in his lived life, and that this author had thrown Muller a filthy look. He said he took this badly. It left him feeling shameful, guilty. So he said he might as well keep writing.

"The ghost of the dead writer - squinting through spectacles, angrily chewing on a smoke. That's all I recall. One of a thousand faces." - I think that's how he'd shaped it. "Oh, and I've got another story for you."

So it turns out Mr Michael Kelly plays golf. The way he hits that Coke can he must have been a real pro. Maybe he played back in Australia. With all the sunshine, and all that space. That would make sense, maybe all Australians hit a coke can that way.

I've come to play with Ambrose (his boy - no real golfer). The three of us, we've come to the park. Not like my park on Telegraph Hill, this park is in Lewisham, an upset park, with cans, and bottles, and glass, and concrete, and a lonely playground. Empty. Just me on my scooter and Ambrose on his bicycle. I'm pretty crazy. More crazy than Ambrose, that's why he likes it when I come down and we go to the park, and we go sick. And that's how it starts... Mr Kelly on a bench, me on my scooter. I have my helmet on, but not on my head, not strapped front-on like a vizor, and I gaze out through the ventilation slits in the helmet. I look like an android. Look damn good. Ambrose and Mr Kelly are both laughing. Mr Kelly is laughing the hardest. Three men walk into the park. And the funny thing is, one of the men, an overgrown man with a moustache and an Adidas tracksuit, well he's holding a golf club, a big one. The other two men are drinking beer. Mum would have crossed the road if she had seen these men. The man with the golf club is the boss. He's cleaner, and the three look funny together. Ambrose looks at his dad. They spend a lot of time in this park, spend a lot of time together...

Ambrose rides to the other end of the park while the men sit down on a park bench. Mr Kelly eases back, and looks more relaxed than usual. Alongside these strangers he looks sharp, like he might have once been a lawyer, or a salesmen, or a detective. He sits there and just smiles. I put my helmet on and start scooting, and Ambrose rides back. The man with the golf club stands up, walks forward with the club on his shoulder, Ambrose appears at my side, brakes on his bike, looks over at his dad. Looks at his Dad angry like, like Mr Kelly has embarrassed Ambrose or done something unforgivable. His cheeks are all red.

Mum always says that Mr Kelly works hard, and he's often tired, tired and stressed: the Kellys have a small house, not much money, and they are always dealing with the neighbours who complain about the noise of their dog, of the baby, of Ambrose, and of their music. They call their neighbour "Davy Bottles", which I think is funny. They call him that because Mr Kelly says he's a miserable drunk, not a fun drunk, always complaining and clinking his bottles in the flat beneath them. I am always careful with Mr Kelly. Mum says he is a poet... Ambrose says he spends his nights working in a bakery. He isn't a very big man, but he has eyes like one of those fighting dogs, those dogs that poor people walk around with, alive and hungry, a dog like a knife - as my dad says.

Maybe all poets look like Mr Kelly?

Maybe all bakers too: those sleepless nights, and the time by the oven, "crazy insomnia" as Ambrose likes to call it.

Whatever it is, the look in his eyes doesn't change when the man makes a move with the golf club. No, Mr Kelly, he turns his head to take a good look. And he nods when his eyes meet those of the man, a long slow nod, like he's half asleep, like they're familiar, but I am sure he has never seen the man. The man with the club is no poet, and certainly no baker.

And then a funny thing happens, the man stops at a Coke can, he lines it up, he does a practice swing, yells "FOURRRR!", and whacks it cleanly, like a real golf pro. And I laugh, and Mr Kelly laughs, and Ambrose looks at his Dad, shakes his head, like he knows something that I don't. And the man turns, looks at Mr Kelly and says, *Sorry, Sir...*

And Mr Kelly replies, *No worries.*

And the man walks back to his friends and mutters under his breath, *He's an Australian.*

And I don't know why he says that, though Mr Kelly *is* an Australian, but it's not important. No, it's more important that he is a baker, and more still that he is a poet, and that he has eyes like a savage dog when he doesn't smile, and if truth told, I'm not entirely comfortable with him. There is something about Mr Kelly, something unpredictable, as if he might just decide to walk off and leave us at the park, leave everything behind.

The man returns, looks at Mr Kelly, new eyes, lines up the can once more, and bang! And Mr Kelly smiles. Ambrose rides back to other end of the park, and I should also, but I want to watch. Good decision because the man turns to Mr Kelly and

asks if he can let me have a swing. And Mr Kelly says, *Sure*.
And I walk over to the man, and Mr Kelly smiles but his eyes
look like the savage dog's, and Ambrose skids up and I can
see he is proper annoyed now, shakes his head. Ambrose
is sure he is smarter than me, he's just like his father. But I
know Ambrose is jealous. He wants to have a go. And the man
shows me how to swing, and I listen, and he shows me how
to hold it, and he holds my hands, and his hands are soft and
oily, but he doesn't have the feel of a bad person. The other
men put their drinks down, and one turns around and looks
around the park. Mr Kelly looks me in the eyes and nods. His
eyes tell me, do it. Mum won't understand any of this when I
get home, she'll just think Mr Kelly has been telling us stories,
filling our heads with ideas.

And then it happens. The man steps back. I swing, and its heavy
and I almost turn three-sixty, and Mr Kelly cries, *Look out!*
And the man ducks, and I just miss his head with the club, and
Mr Kelly laughs, and the man looks at Mr Kelly like he's crazy,
siting on that bench like a gentlemen, and the man walks
away. Ambrose comes and he takes the club, Mr Kelly tells me
to stand back, Ambrose swings, hands me the club, dejected.

I hear some music, music like at Carnival, and the men look
around and at the other end of the park: a car pulls in. The big
man makes his way over to the car... and the two other men
look nervous. And Mr Kelly is standing next to me, and he
gently takes the golf club. *My turn.*

And the big man pauses and looks at Mr Kelly, and Mr Kelly

lines up a can, and I stand back. A rehearsal swing, real slow and smooth, measures his stroke. And then, POW, he hits it. An explosion, the can goes flying in a wind-splitting arc through the air, and the big man, and the men on the bench, and the men in the car, they all stop and stare. I cut the silence with a manic clap.

How did you hit it so hard?

All in the hips.

And then he walks to the can, and the big man walks to the men in the car, and I look back to Mr Kelly. And he is just very calmly lining up a second stroke. I can see Ambrose on his bike, near the bench, where his father had been sitting, and he looks from his father to the men, and back again, shaking his head. And I wonder what is going on. Should we have left the park by now?

The big man makes his way across the park. Mr Kelly nods to acknowledge this as the man draws near, before they look at each other. The big man speaks, says, *Keep the club, the boys might use it, work on their golf.*

And Mr Kelly doesn't smile, he just looks back. And the man gets his friends, and the three clear out.

And that's when Ambrose messes it all up, just when I thought we might be able to keep the club.

What were you doing? Are you out of your mind?

He's almost at the point of tears.

It was better I had the club, says Mr Kelly.

And I don't get it. I do not get it. Why are these Kellys so dramatic? Maybe it's because he's a poet. What's it matter who has the club? And now I can't have it, that's what Mr Michael Kelly tell me. And he does the stupidest thing, he insists on hiding it, all twisted, in a fence, deep in the bushes, where no one will see it. And it will rust.

I know for a fact he didn't attend writing workshops.

Monday had been a bad day. I had been asked to assist in the merchandising of the new store. I moved a lot of cheese. I worked with complete disregard for my body, the way you work when you're beat, when you think there is nothing to be got or to lose. My shoes were coming to pieces. I lost my footing while lifting a wheel of Parmigiano-Reggiano. It was forty kilograms, and I pulled my hamstring. In addition to feeling miserable, I had a dumb limp too. Work is difficult — no, it's impossible — and I can't shake off the desire to leg it and to blow Britain altogether. I am sure I'm not the only one, that this feeling isn't at all unique.

I took the Underground and Overground home, all the time limping and moving awkwardly through the crowds of commuters and travellers, I didn't pick up a copy of the Eventing Standard, not today; the news was shit, bad news, fake news, fake bad new, bad real news, same old shit, same old story, I didn't need a freebie to prove it.

But none of that bullshit was the worst of it. They were all just symptoms of the cause. The cause was a five-month week. It was week three and I was broke. By week two I was stung by a quarterly from Thames Water, and the telephone and internet with BT, Council Tax had gone up, the markets were doing all sorts of crazy shit and my interest rates were through the roof. I was late answering a question from HMRC, and my child benefit was cut. I had to write a letter to Glasgow explaining myself, and provide documents from my little one's doctor, proving that she existed, and I had to pay ten quid even for that. It was a farce. I wondered, why the fuck isn't anyone talking about a revolution? No, everyone was busy trying to poke a finger in the eye of Europe, glaring at foreigners on the Tube. The situation was dire. And the one in charge, a difficult human she promised to be, as if that was what the world needed, as if anyone gave a shit, or knew what the government were doing, and what all these fucking changes meant, or at the very least where the country was actually leaving for, that it wasn't wandering aimlessly.

I got home. And that was a relief.

That previous Sunday night we'd had a chicken for dinner, a real treat, roasted with spuds, with some flatbread I'd made while drinking BB9, just about the best beer in the world. That evening I boiled the white bones of the chicken, with just a sprig of thyme, an onion, and two cloves of crushed garlic. I could imagine the chook, the carcass was so thin and spindly, its bones were more like those of a reasonably large and super weird mutant fish... it must have been a bird beyond a battery hen, a kind of high-rise roosting matchbox hen squeezed in with countless others, I guess featherless, tortured, bored out of their brains, staring out between thin wire bars, staring out at a thousand other chickens in the same predicament, the ruckus of all those birds clucking at once. Imagine. We were at least showing the bird some respect, boiling the spindly bones down to nothing, chucking the grey remains to the dog. I had read some diatribe in a trade magazine that bone broths and marrow were all the rage. The very rich will go to no end to replicate the dietary condition of poor.

When I got home the house stunk like boiled chicken. My Missus had started making risotto with the stock, and it was boiling away like a bad memory, we were short on the right kind of rice so she cut the Alborio with Jasmine, in the end, there wasn't much in it just rice and grey chicken. I limped to the table with my steaming bowl, I dusted it with Parmigiano cut with table cheddar. No wine or beer, black tea and loads of white sugar. I'll say it again, five-week months suck. They never used to suck this much. The writing is on the wall, we are all on credit eating boiled down chicken, all except for the super-rich and the hangers-on, and half of them are starving themselves in imitation of the poor, decked out in shiny finery, trying to stay beautiful. What happened?

It was a cold night and everyone was eager for bed: wife, children, the whole damn world. I couldn't bring myself to sleep, I settled down with Grossman's 'Life & Fate', some poor bastard was going on about the Kulaks, and saboteurs, and I wasn't so sure about the saboteurs, but someone was getting the better of us all, even now, seventy years on. Those damn Kulaks. Those damn Tsars. Those bankers. Those politicians. Those masters of the deal. The deal... lorded over us.

The next morning I made my way to the office. The site manager, György, a Bulgarian from Varna, was in a state of high anxiety. The cause being his trials, mostly difficulties finalising his application for permanent residency, this was prudent measure on his part to ease the fear of leaving the country even for a holiday, being stuck abroad "without my papers." I had heard the boys talking about the paperwork - seventy pages of bullshit. György was a good worker, a sure thing, he wasn't going anywhere, and the residency confirmed this. More and more the promotions were going to the British in the company, no questions asked, most of us figured that this was a reflection of the cold realisation of management that the rest of us might up and go, if we weren't booted out, or simply discouraged from staying - it all amounted to the same thing.

Anyhow, it was a big day, another part of town and a new shop opening. A new story, or chapter, or something for the company. So, first things first, I went to the production kitchen and made sure everything was in shipshape. The ops man marched into my office and started going on about how the owner Mr M wanted - no, required - no, insisted - on everything being perfect, not just perfect, no, but *bloody* perfect. He had a particularly painful high pitched voice as if his balls were mid-drop. And for the umpteenth time that day the kitchen was invaded by middle-management trying to terrify everything into order: it wasn't yet 6.30AM. I had decided to head for the new shop when it opened and to avoid the high drama. The driver came, *if it's not Piotr too late it's Piotr too early*, I liked to say. He couldn't put a foot right with management, and particularly the ops man. The ops man, always crying out for Piotr: *Where is he? Why is he here now? no, he's late, no, he's early*, etc. etc. We got in the van, and we raced about town. He put his classical music on, which was better than Ed Sheerbastard.

And the new store was in a state of uproar. There was a monumental bread disaster concerning one supplier, amongst the vegetables five products were missing tickets, and worse still the fruit and veg hadn't been fully displayed, and the staff didn't have aprons and badges. As for the merchandising manager (a young hack promoted by the ops man to advance the ops man's ambitions), well he was getting in everyone's way, hand in pockets, face breaking out in spots, and all the time him blundering about nervously. I wondered, was he fucking stoned? And even Mr M had come down from the Cotswolds and was blustering around, making everyone scared shitless, dressed like he was fresh from some covert hunt. The clock was moving perilously, and the customers weren't allowed in, and there was a line outside like it was a new iPhone launch, and the doors just couldn't be opened until everything was perfect, and I wondered about those weird customers, didn't they have something else to do, those sick bastards. And it opened with a bang.

Mr M took us - us being the main players - to a cafe for a debrief. There he settled into his allocated role, shifted to instruction, and authority, his sense of isolation in the world and amongst others only broken by the execution of authority, I imagined his folk had done it for a thousand years or more. Shop 19 would be opening soon, in 6 weeks! We would need to make notes while our ideas were fresh, to record all our wrongs like a confessional. I was meant to be meeting a winemaster for a tasting, I sent her a message apologising for the delay - this business could go on till lunchtime. There was the ops guy, six members from the PR department, the merchandising manager (that poor sod), marketing, and Mr M's assistant who was carrying Mr M's golf clubs, fuck knows why. I had only eaten the last half a box of Italian biscuits (samples that had been sent to my office on the previous day) since morning. Menus were laid while each of the us that wasn't me studied their mobiles, sending messages, answering messages, checked facts and figures from the previous day, everyone busying themselves in an attempt to suggest they were busy. I studied the menu, my eyes rested on eggs Benedict, the waiter asked what we'd like. Everyone paused. Mr M answered.

Green Tea, his eyes dropped to the menu again, I won't have anything else, giving his cue. Maybe he had a round to play that afternoon.

I pondered ordering scrambled eggs, settled on liquid. The meeting was a bore. No victories, just the usual criticisms, the usual plan for a quick fix. We had been here before, and we realised the futility of good results and the implications of failure. All apart from the ops man, who was like some ancient eunuch. He bought into it in totality, right into the company, his boss, his role. It was better to eat boiled up battery hens, and hope for a getaway or something close. Or something fucking close...

I was the first to grow restless with the conversation. I took my leave. I rushed out the door with the appearance of being in a hurry, being very busy, committed. I turned a corner and limped to the station. In approximately thirty minutes I was at Highbury, and straight up the hill, late for my tasting with the very celebrated winemaster. She had twelve bottles laid out, glasses, spittoons, tasting notes. I asked her if she had a calculator - she got me one (*the shit you ask for!*). It was evident that I was exhausted, and she was more than astute enough to gather this. The tasting was constructive, and plans were laid for a spring and summer range. I didn't approach the meeting with any real gusto, the energy I might have had at week two on a four week month when I was rested, well-fed, and agreeable. I declined the tasting of two very good wines (the winemaster's favourites), I had tasted the wines, the very same vintages, only recently. And the winemaster insisted on me taking the wines in a box. That at least would be pleasing! I would have something to drink that night, and a second bottle I could give to one of the other workers.

Limping with the box I made my way back down the hill. I jumped on the first train and switched from line to line en route to Sloane Square. I would go straight to the office and check emails, make phone calls.

On the platform at Sloane Square the usual crowd was exiting, west Londoners in the main. A lady stopped me, a not so old woman, in very fine attire, physically striking. I am in truth not so very fancy, but what does that mean, and does it matter?

She asked abruptly, with an air of authority, *Would you have the time?*

We had been in the carriage together. I sat the box down with the bottles of wine, she fidgeted and irritably studied me. The bulk of the passengers cleared the platform. I pulled my phone from my pocket.

One o'clock.

I picked the box up, we both started walking side by side, both moving quickly towards the exit.

Do you work here? She asked, harshly, with frustration. I was in old trousers and wearing a tired coat, carrying my box. I didn't look like the people in the neighbourhood, the people on the platform. This wasn't my part of town, yet there was nothing to indicate that I worked at the station. In fact, I had been in a carriage with the woman and exited with her. The two of us were passengers, just the same.

Pardon?

Do you work here?

I studied her, and I could see the anger in her eyes, a faint glow like the onset of a rash on her dull, thin, swan-like neck. She needed the question answered, it would relate to other questions and requirements that would need to be met, and met immediately.

Are you a Kulak? I asked.

Pardon?

Are you a Kulak?

What on earth are you talking about?

I asked, are you a Kulak? That class of peasant that the communist reviled, and Stalin did his very best to eliminate.

And I turned and made my way out of the station, and hurried to my office and my desk, all the time limping, and everyone in the office wanted reports on the new shop. The truth was they were all excited by a second box of wines that someone had left on my desk. I shook my head. What I would have given for some lamb, or bread, or potatoes, or cheese in the way of samples. And then Piotr the driver came through and I palmed him a bottle.

Suck on one of those bad boys, and tell me what you think.

A pro, I is the real pro, he replied with a wink.

And then György, that hack, stumbled in and tried to work out if something was amiss, still miserable, and still dreaming about his British residency, and that did it.

Fuck the residency, pal, I slung that miserable son of a bitch a bottle. It was at 3 o'clock, and time to jack it in. Work. Britain. All the bullshit. Time to jack it in.

Here's the thing.

I don't even think he's actually a Tadhg. Maybe he's not even a Muller? What I've started to consider is that even though I think that, I don't know it. Maybe it's all real. All of it. Tadhg Muller is an odd name for a Tasmanian of Irish Catholic descent, is it not? But it doesn't mean he isn't Tadhg. And it doesn't mean Muller's memoirs, here, in lieu of a novelette, mean one particular thing about anything. The reality of this autofiction is his darkness, its London. [This] is what he wants to write. I've let some of the light in, he's let some of it out.

The lights were off when I entered, they'd been off for three years. Still, he was looking out, the door buzzed open before I put a hand to it, this was a change. And inside, a window so slightly open, and a breeze stirring the air, and soft natural light. Three years is a long time, the fresh air was good, three years of life in the darkness, like a crab, or insect, stuck under a stone.

The mould spores... he grumbles as he stares back with his heavy-lidded eyes, a nod to the window.

Yes, the air is good, maybe he was getting better? Maybe he'd had enough? Maybe just mould spores after all.

I tell him of my small success, that I will be having a novel published, on the smallest print run in the universe. I drum the arm of my chair impatiently with two fingers.

He'd known me when the chips were down. When I kept a chair at the table, even while losing, even when I didn't have a card to play - in this way we are different.

Which one? he asks.

Which what?

You know, which book?

Oh, the one where you're the hero, I shrug, and realising my error, I make to steer the conversation elsewhere. *Visitors?*

Visitors! You kidding? He shakes his head, very slowly, like a dinosaur might move its ginormous head. I guess it's the spine, the bones. It is a painful movement.

He informs me that there has been no visitors since I was last in town. My efforts had never been great. I came when I could, passing through, passing through for the cash, the odd job. He'd been sick a long time, midway through must have been when I left, droves of people were clearing out. Who wouldn't leave? Someone too afraid to move, or somebody stuck.

This bloke didn't want anyone to come, he'd had his dose of charity. Me, well I enjoyed his conversation. But secretly, I am also selfish, there is a refuge in this place - in his private hell. Though I would be lying if I didn't concede that it's a hard job to sit here, to look upon his face, to have his world staring back at you, to not feel the pang of guilt, and pang of relief when you are done talking and you shut the door behind you, go back to life. He doesn't look so good these days. It's not just the eyes. The flesh has dropped from his handsome face, the cheeks are sunken and cavernous, his bones are prominent and poke out through tired clothes, just like a coat hanger would, and the hair on his tense skull is patchy, as it is on his face, like a sci-fi hero, a radioactive villain, a mutant hero in the making.

Once he was the darling of the neighbourhood, he had lovers, friends (a whole crowd of pals), I only met him on my own (unless, in the old days, we chanced upon the boys), he always had me down as an oddity: poor, children, young, no prospects, the only person he knew who bothered to hold down a job, maybe? In the old days, he was always calling by, making sure the kids were alright, that we weren't going to pieces. Mostly, then, I was broke, out of luck, a long time out of luck, a long time struggling to turn luck around.

He scratches his face and turns his eyes to me.

Does it have a name?

Everything got a name, Al, I sigh.

And?

What do you mean, and? I reply. *You might read the thing, and you might not like what you read... and you don't read anyway. Fuck.. you tell me you forget a page as soon as you've read it.*

Hmm...

Precisely, a wave of my hand.

At what point does my story begin? He asks.

Your story? I roll my eyes. *Jesus... is that how it is?*

I'm a minor character? His voice a little quiet now, his voice almost tender.

It's not your collapse, it's your glory days.

Oh... his bony finger across his chin, *my glory days?* An injured note to the voice.

It's nothing, really, it's nothing.

Afghanistan? His voice is soft now like we are playing a guessing game, a guessing game where he will arrive at an answer through a series of yes and noes, a game I might play with my son or my daughter: What Is It? or Who Am I? Something like that. I don't know if it has a name. Everything has a name. Does his condition have a name? Everything has a name, even that bloody book.

No. Not in Afghanistan, I answer.

Have I passed through Europe...

God...

Am I in a kitchen?

Glory days, I said. *Glory.*

Are my qualifications recognised?

Your qualifications! I laugh. *You're more than a statistic,* I remark as a matter of fact, like I am challenging something, a perception, a feeling, an ingrained view, the negation of an actual life, a real life just like yours and mine.

A no or a yes?

A maybe mate. Maybe.

Nah, come on. There's no sign of ill health? Or mental shock? Trauma? Come on!

All things pass, I answer.

Do they? Where did that come from? Are you being smart?

No, one way or the other... all things pass. Everything.

Just like that, he shakes his head.

Maybe.

Another clue?

A statement mate... a statement.

Agh, that's a yes.

No answer.

He starts again, hot on my tail. *Surely I've suffered a mental collapse, trauma, I am very sick? As the hero. Like I am a... what is it... you know, an antihero.*

Life and art, they're not the same, I tell him. *Not the same at all. Everyone knows that.*

They look alike.

Life looks stranger.

For a time he was homeless, out on the streets, crashing out at other people's places, that was when his mental health took a turn. The loss of a sense of place. We lost contact. I didn't have his address, nor a number. I was on the move. When I passed by I saw people in the neighbourhood, the news was bad - no not bad - bloody awful. Mostly everyone avoided him, or forgot him, mostly they stayed away. Maybe they just couldn't face him, they were a hopeless bunch, passing life by in the old neighbourhood, eternally young minded and growing old bodied, holding up the bars, chasing girls half their age, watching the football, talking nonsense, pontificating. Mates at the watering hole in Ladbroke Grove

Finally, I got his address. At that point, I had a job... had had a job for months. When I found him he had deteriorated dramatically, he didn't leave his room, had serious issues with light, chronic pains in his back, his jaw had partially collapsed, cranial problems, the works. He was debilitated. Even now the changes aren't much, the picture mostly the same, this won't be a happy-ever-after story, there isn't a good ending.

I see your curtains are drawn, I change the topic again.

He puts a hand on the table and places a pair of Sidewinders over his eyes, and does it very slowly like he has arthritis, which he may do, or something similar, a condition that afflicts the elderly, anyway.

Nice, I say.

Want them?

If I'm not careful he'll make me take those shades. He walks to the window, and opens it, the light catches the dust, he picks up a hoody from the sofa, and with a faint shiver pulls it over his head, lowering the hood to the tip of his shades.

Happy now? he looks out the window.

You look like Tyson Fury.

Who's that?

A boxer. Had a hard time too.

So the book.

Oh for fuck's sake!

Just answer my question.

I told you, it's you, or at least a hero based on you, a sketch of you... what more?

Yes, I get that. But... my glory days?

We pause and look at each other. The question is very important, more important than the book, the book is irrelevant, the seed is what matters. His persistence marks a change. Mostly, in the past, we have sat in silence. Usually he lists his complaints, recounts the problems he's been having with a particular psychologist, or a doctor. He details the detrimental impact of medication on muscle and bone, details his attempt to get off the medication, details being trapped in a bed, in a room, details being suicidal, suicidal for days on end, suicidal night after night. And the painful stories of other people's attempts to appear to care, the awkwardness of their compassion, mostly their need to detail their own misery, and the bad stories this provides. To his benefit, he always tells me that everything is relative, his pains can't be measured against other people's, vis-à-vis. I swear he's wrong, his pain is different, different from someone who has lost a boyfriend, a job, or is feeling lost in a career, putting away too much booze, being demented at the thought of growing old and getting saggy tits, a beer gut, wrinkles, hair loss, going grey, impotency, not falling in love, not having made a baby, not having sired an heir... the things I guess you might think when you wake up and time caught you out, that you've actually grown old in this town, old like you never expected, at least not so old so soon, and not so alone. No, his problems aren't that regular. His is a loss of place, of belonging, of home, and much, much more, adrift in the world, shipwrecked here, as good as beat, washed up, stranded.

You'll never read the thing. The truth is it's a heap of shit, I mutter.

I'm sure it's not.

So, it's you in the future. This is all done. This shit is all done, I wave my hand to signal something imaginary, *the room, the world, his troubles, life. Maybe even all the bloody wars.*

I'm the Buddha, he laughs, he actually fucking laughs.

Yeah, when you're the fucking Buddha.

That's a start, he adds.

Too right, I say.

The fact and fiction of his life have pulverised into tragedies. I pass by, a witness of what? The room is his entire world, every last crack, every corner. He is a worthy hero, I lower my head.

A deep guilt falls over me, with shame, sadness, helplessness, real helplessness like there is nothing I can do about anything. He is fading out, I don't see where this will end, I don't see how much he can take. I can feel my eyes well up.

Aside from what he wants and what canards he wants to disseminate, there were actual rumours about Tadhg, too. The said London had taken its toll on him, like it does for so many, and that fucking pissed me off.

I couldn't find a way to argue against it, but I didn't want that to be "Tadhg Muller". And then when I got him to sign a contract for this book, and he signed it "Muller", he said, "I bought something to seal the deal," and handed me a saucisson from his little French town. "Any deal worth making should be sealed with a sausage."

Sounds like some read. He smiles. *Well done,* and he thrusts out a hand with a sympathetic air. I lift my head, there is the weight of iron in that hand. I begin to laugh, and he joins me. There is a break in the clouds, the sun streams in. I lean back and smile, he draws the curtains, it's time for the road, to get home, wherever home is.

Acknowledgements

Preston, Edwards, and K.J Muller, thanks for the encouragement, patience, and help, and for giving your time. And Keith Botsford, for insightful correspondence at just the right time.

Seeta, Hector, and Paloma, XXXX for everything else.

The stories in this novelette first appeared as standalone short stories in:

1. Skive Literary Magazine (Australia), 2011

Crack The Spine (USA), Issue Thirty Two, 2012

2. Open Pen Magazine (UK), Issue Six, 2012

3. Island Magazine (Australia), 2013

4. Southerly Journal (Australia), 2014

5. Island Magazine (Australia), 2015

6. 'Islands and Cities' (Transportation Press), 2015

7. 'The Open Pen Anthology' (Limehouse Books), 2016

8. Lost Lit Magazine (UK), 2017

9. Confluence (UK), 2018

The poem "Sydney" that appears on P23 and P24 is written by Konrad Muller.

The "editorial notes" in this novelette are unlikely to be written by